A Foal is Born

words by Hans-Heinrich Isenbart / photographs by Hanns-Jörg Anders

translated by Catherine Edwards

G. P. PUTNAM'S SONS   NEW YORK

First American Edition 1976
Text and illustrations copyright © 1975 Reich Verlag
English translation copyright © 1976 by G. P. Putnam's Sons
All rights reserved. Published
simultaneously in Canada by Longman
Canada, Limited, Toronto.
PRINTED IN THE UNITED STATES OF AMERICA
04208

Library of Congress Cataloging in Publication Data
Isenbart, Hans-Heinrich.
A foal is born.
Translation of Ein Fohlen kommt zur Welt.
SUMMARY: Describes the birth and first few hours of a foal.
1. Horses—Juvenile literature.   2.   Animals, Infancy
of—Juvenile literature.   3.   Parturition—Juvenile literature.
[1. Horses.   2.   Animals—Infancy]
I. Anders, Hanns-Jörg.   II.   Title.
SF302.I78   1976   636.1'07   76-2605
ISBN 0-399-20517-9   ISBN 0-399-61006-5 lib. bdg.

A Foal is Born

A herd of horses grazes in the sunshine. Because they live in a southern land where it is always warm, the herd is kept outside all year round.

One of the mares in the herd is about to give birth to a baby horse, a foal. The foal's father is a handsome black stallion.

For the past 330 days, almost a full year, the foal, so tiny at first, has been growing inside its mother.

Now it is ready to be born.

Inside the mare, the foal has been lying on his back within a sac. Now he turns onto his stomach with his head facing the rear of his mother.

The foal will be pushed down a narrow channel and out into the world. Before the foal starts down the channel, a bubble of water goes ahead of him. The bubble helps stretch the

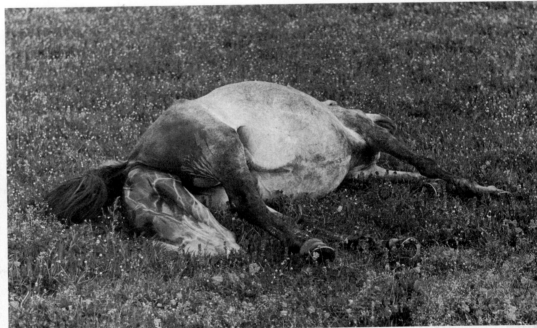

channel. When it has passed out completely, the sac holding the foal starts to come out of the mare. First, comes the head, then the forelegs. You can see them inside the sac.

The little foal sleeps as soundly as he slept inside his mother.

Daylight drifts into the sac. Usually foals are
born in the evening, but here the birth is during the
day, so it is easy to see what is happening.

The light wakes up the foal, and as soon as
he moves, the sac rips open.

Although the mare and her foal are still bound together by a cord called the umbilical cord, the foal can move himself. Bothered by the bright sun in his eyes, he turns his head.

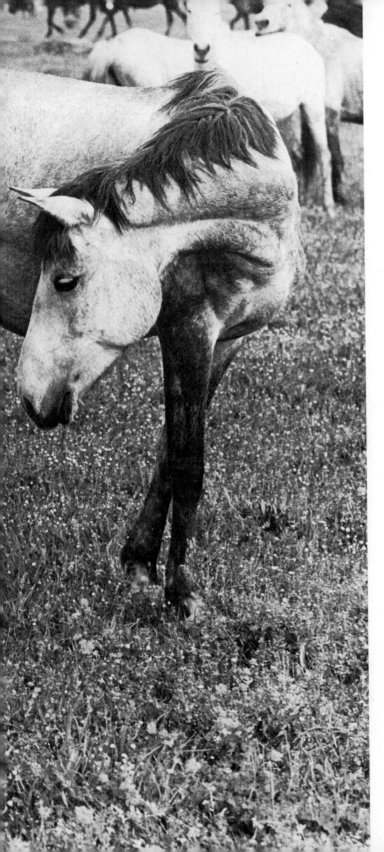

Inside his mother, the foal was fed food through the cord, but it's not needed any longer. The mare stands up, and as she does, the cord is ripped apart.

The foal wiggles out of the sac. He's too weak and tired to stand up. His mother watches over him. She will look after her foal with all the care and concern of a mother for her newborn baby.

Still bothered by the light, the foal lies in the grass, swaying his head. He is wet and cold. Everything has happened so quickly.

It is only fifteen minutes since the foal was
pushed out of the darkness and warmth inside his
mother. Above him her warm breath, her soft mouth,
and her dry, massaging tongue make him feel alive.

But he's not really awake yet. Under his mother's warm nostrils, he sinks sleepily back onto the grass.

Then he raises his head and looks about.

Surely for the little foal, the first look around
must be overwhelming. We don't know this
for sure, but we can imagine.

The other horses gather around to look. They
form a protective circle and begin to help lick him
dry. The foal is well taken care of by the herd.

Large, gentle faces reach down to the foal.
Soft noses, warm breaths, and firm tongues
massage the wet hide. The foal can smell different
scents. He smells the sun-warmed grass. He smells
the other horses. He is part of the herd, and he has
learned this right away.

Although this little foal has been born outdoors
in the midst of a herd, most foals are born in stables.
There people, instead of other horses, stand by the
mare and help rub the foal dry with straw. Even
in a stall, a foal will look around for the herd.

The little foal is still very tired. His ears droop,
and he needs the care, protection, and closeness
of his mother and the other horses.

The foal feels safe near his mother.
She is cleaning him with her tongue, especially
around the nose. There is still some fluid from
birth in his nostrils which can make it hard
for the foal to breathe.

The other horses keep washing him, too.

While the nose cleaning is going on, the foal gets to know his mother and the other horses. He uses both his eyes and his nose. Horses depend on smell much more than we do. Later the young horse will recognize his mother over long distances.

While the mare is drying his hide,
the foal tries to stand up, a difficult job!

A foal can stand and walk around only a
few hours after being born. When you and I
were born, we could only lie in a crib at
first and then sit up. It was almost a
year before we could walk on our own.

A strong, healthy foal will try to get
up only a half hour after birth. He must,
because in a wild herd the horses are often
on the move. They may have to go on to new
grazing lands or flee some danger. A herd
will wait only a short time for a foal to
follow. If the foal is too weak or too
young to keep up, it gets left behind.
Sometimes the mother lingers with her foal.
But eventually she must join the herd.
This is nature's way.

This foal is healthy.

But standing
by himself is hard.

He is still so small and weak. His legs so long. But he will make it!

He tries to untangle his long legs. One leg keeps getting in the way of another. It's hard to balance when the front leg is up and then it's down!

He's almost up. . .   then he's down!

The forelegs look right. Now up with
a swing. Down he goes again. No one helps.
His mother waits. The foal must do it
by himself.

He tries leaning against his mother's
legs. If only his legs weren't weak.
Now his mother's stomach is in the way.

At last! He's up.

A little bowlegged and weak, the foal stands for the first time.

How quickly he is steady! After a short time, he can stand, walk, and run easily.

The foal takes a look around him. He is about ready to take his place in the herd. His eyes are bright. He can point his ears. He wants to look at everything.

His long, stiltlike legs stand firm as his mother stays beside him. He feels her closeness, and this makes him brave. Everything is so new, the grass, the flowers, and even the other horses. He is part of the herd. A strong little horse that can make his own way.

Now he is hungry. He looks for milk. It will be both food and medicine for him. His mother's milk will keep him healthy and protect him from getting sick.

When he has had enough milk, he looks at the other horses. They smell differently from his mother. He goes from one to another sniffing. Soon he can tell each one by its smell.

But everything
is so new and
exhausting.
It's time
to rest. . . .

For the first two or three weeks, the foal
will drink his mother's milk. Then he will start
nibbling at blades of grass.

Often he plops down and falls fast asleep.
There is so much to see and learn in the beginning
that he tires quickly. But with good food and rest
he will soon grow strong.

A foal is born. How astounding it is to watch a tiny foal be born and stand within a few hours, ready to live and grow and run with the herd.